This book belongs to

_____

_____

_____

_____

Age _____

TREASURY
OF FAVOURITE
TALES

© 2014 Alligator Books
Published by Alligator Books
Gadd House, Arcadia Avenue
London N3 2JU

Printed in China 12285

TREASURY OF FAVOURITE TALES

The Three Billy Goats Gruff

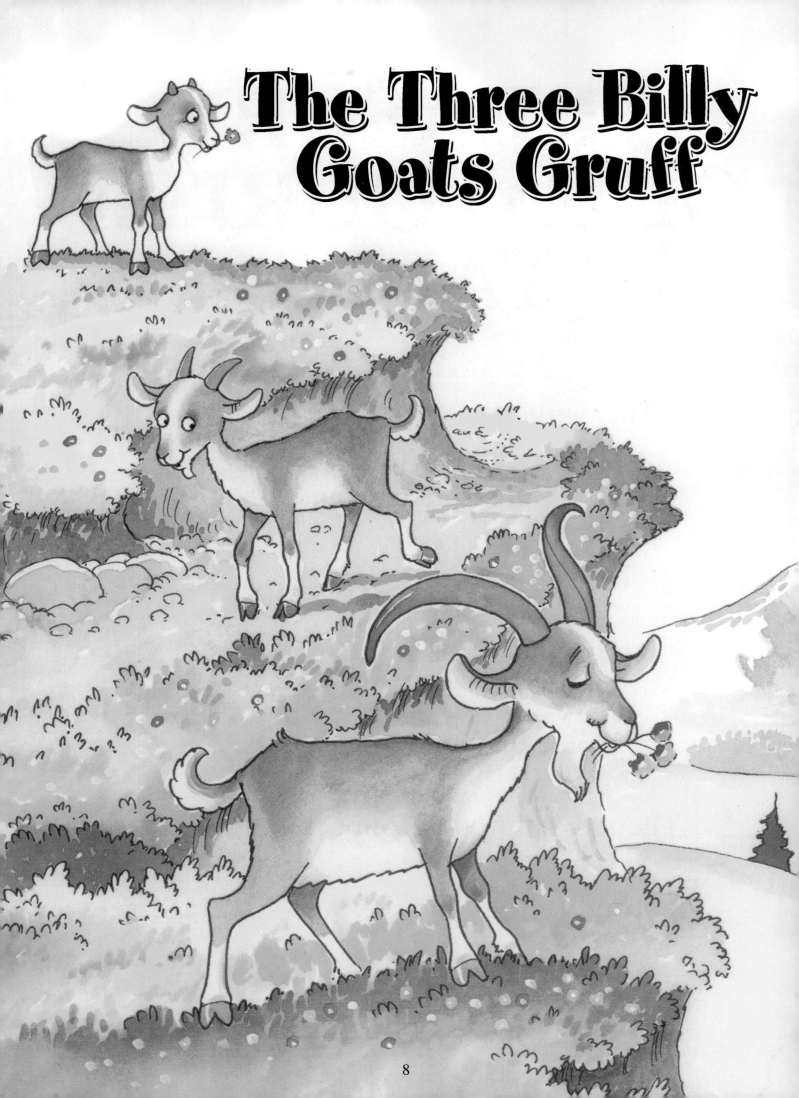

Once upon a time there were three billy goats. First there was the little billy goat Gruff, who was the smallest of the three.

Then there was the middle billy goat Gruff, who was bigger than the little billy goat Gruff, but not as big as the great big billy goat Gruff.

And he was, as you can see, the biggest of them all!

Now these billy goats lived in a tiny village at the foot of a high mountain.

Every year during spring and summer, the three billy goats Gruff left their tiny village and went to stay up on the hillside nearby.

All day long they nibbled the juicy green grass that grew there, and by night they slept underneath the stars.

Some days the three billy goats Gruff crossed the river to the other side of the valley, where the grass was even greener and juicier and full of sweet-smelling wild flowers.

Now the bridge over the river was very rickety-rackety. It swayed and creaked and went wibbly-wobbly.

"Perhaps someone will mend it one fine day," said the three billy goats Gruff every time they went trip-trapping across.

But when winter came along and snow covered the juicy green grass, the three billy goats Gruff said goodbye to the hillside, and went back to live in their tiny village at the foot of the high mountain.

So every year before the weather got too cold and the snow was too deep, the three billy goats Gruff trotted home down the mountain track.

The folks in the village were delighted to see them, especially the children. For it was their job to look after the three billy goats Gruff during the long months of winter.

Sometimes the children gave them oats to nibble from a basket, and barley from a big brass bucket.

The little billy goat Gruff, as you can see, would nibble anything that came his way!

But the three billy goats Gruff were happiest of all when the children brought them sweet-smelling hay. It reminded them of the juicy green grass that grew on the hillside in springtime.

And through the long dark winter nights, when the three billy goats Gruff were nice and warm and cosy in the barn, the children would listen to stories.

When the shutters were closed tight and the fire was burning brightly, that was the time the children wanted to hear about...TROLLS!

Now there are trolls with claws and rows of teeth!
There are trolls with horns and great big feet!
Some of them are scaly! Some of them are hairy!
But every single troll is...BIG, BAD AND SCARY!

The children listened to tales of trolls until it was past their bedtime.

"Goodnight and beware of the big bad trolls," they whispered sleepily as they went off to bed.

They hide under bridges,
In dark caves and holes.
Don't go up the mountain,
For fear of the TROLLS!

Now the three billy goats Gruff never heard the tales that were told about the trolls on dark winter nights.

Which was just as well perhaps!

On winter nights, as soon as darkness fell, all the animals in the warm cosy barn settled down to sleep.

The three billy goats Gruff closed their eyes and dreamed of spring, when the juicy green grass would grow on the hillside once more.

Then one very special morning, as the three billy goats Gruff came out of the barn...something felt different!

Birds were whistling, bees were humming and a sunbeam tickled the little billy goat Gruff's nose...SPRING HAD COME AT LAST!

"I can smell spring!" and the middle billy goat Gruff sighed as he sniffed the fresh air.

"It must be the new juicy green grass on the hillside you can smell!" said the great big billy goat Gruff.

So, without wasting a single moment, the three of them trotted out of the tiny village, and turned up the narrow path that led to the hillside.

When the three billy goats Gruff saw the new grass, it made them feel hungry, and they began to nibble the fresh shoots straight away.

They chomped and they munched, they chewed and they crunched all morning long, until every single bit of the juicy green grass had vanished.

"Where's it all gone?" gasped the little billy goat Gruff as he stared at the ground.

"We've eaten it, I'm afraid!" said the middle billy goat Gruff sadly.

"Look across the river!" cried the great big billy goat Gruff. "There's a whole hillside covered with new juicy green grass over there!"

17

The three billy goats Gruff could hardly wait to cross over the bridge and get to the new juicy green grass on the other side.

"I wonder if the bridge is still rickety-rackety?" asked the little billy goat Gruff as they rushed down to the river.

"I wonder if the bridge still sways and creaks and goes wibbly-wobbly?" asked the middle billy goat Gruff.

"I wonder if our hooves still go trip-trap every time we cross the bridge?" asked the great big billy goat Gruff.

"I'm the smallest! I'll go first!" called the little billy goat Gruff. "Then we'll find out!"

And off he went.

Now the three billy goats Gruff didn't know that during the long cold dark months of winter, a BIG BAD TROLL had come to live beneath the rickety-rackety bridge.

The instant he heard the little billy goat Gruff's small hooves trip-trapping across the wibbly-wobbly wooden planks, the big bad troll leapt out from under the rickety-rackety bridge.

He raged! He roared! He showed his claws!

He gnashed his pointed teeth!

"I'll eat anyone I catch trip-trapping across my bridge!" he growled fiercely.

The little billy goat Gruff stood quite still. He did not shake! He did not quake! He did not scream or shiver!

Instead he looked at the big bad troll and said, "My brother is much bigger than me. He'll make a better supper!"

So the big bad troll let the little billy goat Gruff go. And he went trip-trapping across the rickety-rackety bridge to the other side.

And there he stayed munching the juicy green grass as he waited for his brothers.

Next to cross the rickety-rackety bridge was the middle billy goat Gruff, who was bigger than the little billy goat Gruff, but not as big as the great big billy goat Gruff.

The very instant the big bad troll heard the middle billy goat's hooves trip-trapping across the wibbly-wobbly wooden planks, he leapt out from under the rickety-rackety bridge.

He raged! He roared! He showed his claws! He gnashed his pointed teeth!

"I'll eat anyone I catch trip-trapping across my bridge!" he growled fiercely.

The middle billy goat Gruff stood quite still. He didn't shake! He didn't quake! He didn't scream or shiver!

Instead he looked at the big bad troll and said, "My brother is much bigger than me. He'll make a better supper!"

So the big bad troll let the middle billy goat Gruff go. And he went trip-trapping across the rickety-rackety bridge to the other side.

And there he stayed munching the juicy green grass as he waited for his great big brother.

Now the big bad troll had made such a din, and hollered so loudly, that the great big billy goat Gruff realised what was happening.

And he knew just what to do!

The instant the big bad troll heard the great big billy goat Gruff's hooves on the wibbly-wobbly wooden planks, he leapt up onto the rickety-rackety bridge.

Then he opened his mouth wide and yelled, "You're big enough for my supper!"

"Oh no, I'm not!" snorted the great big billy goat Gruff.

Then he put down his huge sharp horns and he charged CRASH! BANG! WHAM!

The big bad troll whizzed high into the air, then flew over the mountains roaring and hollering. Where he landed, I can not tell, but he never came back again!

When the folks in the tiny village learned that the big bad troll had gone for ever, they wanted to thank the billy goats Gruff for being so brave and clever.

So they decided to celebrate.

It was the children's idea to have a grand picnic in honour of the three billy goats Gruff.

And everybody agreed.

So the next afternoon, (when the rickety-rackety bridge had been mended at last!) everyone trooped over the river to the hillside. The three billy goats Gruff ate plenty of oats and barley.

And the big bad troll, wherever he landed, must have told all the other trolls...never, never, under any circumstances whatsoever, go near the three billy goats Gruff!

The End

The Gingerbread Man

Once there lived an old man, an old woman and a little boy who all lived together in a country cottage. The old woman had been baking bread, cakes and sweet crunchy biscuits all morning. She had a bit of dough left over, so she decided to make a Gingerbread Man.

The little boy was very keen to help. Straight away
he rolled up his sleeves, and very carefully, he gave the
Gingerbread Man currants for eyes, a bright red cherry
nose, a smiley orange slice mouth and three buttons made
of fat juicy raisins.

The old woman popped the Gingerbread Man into the
oven to bake, then she went outside to talk to the old man
in the garden.

All of a sudden, the oven door burst open and out leapt
the Gingerbread Man. To the little boy's amazement, he ran
across the kitchen floor and out of the open door.

The little boy could hardly believe his eyes as the Gingerbread Man raced down the garden path.

"Look at our Gingerbread Man!" yelled the little boy. "He's running away!"

"Be quick and catch him before he reaches the garden gate!" cried the old man.

"I'll grab him, then we'll eat him at once!" shouted the old woman.

So the old woman, the old man and the little boy all began to chase after the Gingerbread Man.

But the Gingerbread Man was far too quick for them.
He'd escaped from the hot oven and now he was free as
a bird.

As he ran through the gate and down the lane, the
Gingerbread Man laughed and yelled at the top of his
voice.

"Run! Run! As fast as you can! You can't catch me,
I'm the Gingerbread Man!"

A snappy spotted dog, that lived at the end of the lane,
saw the runaway Gingerbread Man and joined in the chase.

When the Gingerbread Man saw the snappy spotted dog, he ran faster than ever.

"If I catch you first, I'll gobble you up, I promise!" barked the snappy spotted dog.

When the old man, the old woman and the little boy heard this, they ran faster too. They didn't want to lose their tasty golden Gingerbread Man with the red cherry nose, the currant eyes and juicy raisin buttons.

So they carried on down the lane chasing after the Gingerbread Man.

A hungry black crow flying overhead saw the Gingerbread Man, and swooped down hoping to take a big bite. But the Gingerbread Man was far too quick for him, and jumped out of his way.

"I've outrun an old man, an old woman, a little boy, a snappy spotted dog...and now you!" the Gingerbread Man yelled to the crow.

"Run! Run! As fast as you can! You can't catch me, I'm the Gingerbread Man!"

At the end of the lane was a field where three mowers were busy cutting corn, and raking it into neat piles to dry.

When they saw the Gingerbread Man running past, they stopped working at once and joined in the chase.

"Stop little Gingerbread Man!" cried one of the mowers. "You look tasty enough to eat for our lunch."

"I'll eat his head!" puffed the first mower.

"I'll eat his arms!" panted the second.

"And I'll eat both his legs!" gasped the third.

But the Gingerbread Man didn't stop. He skipped and danced as he crossed the corn field, and he called back to the three mowers...

"Run! Run! As fast as you can! You can't catch me, I'm the Gingerbread Man!"

The midday sun was so hot, and the mowers felt so tired, they sat down in the shade to eat their lunch. They ate bread and cheese, but no tasty Gingerbread Man, of course!

How the old man, the old woman, the little boy and the snappy spotted dog longed to stop and rest in the shade, but they were all determined to carry on and catch the Gingerbread Man.

They ran up hill and down dale. They ran over bridges, through woods and across fields. Everyone had come so far, they were all exhausted and quite out of breath.

But the Gingerbread Man wasn't tired at all, and he sang at the top of his voice as he raced along.

"Run! Run! As fast as you can! You can't catch me, I'm the Gingerbread Man!"

And he was absolutely right. The Gingerbread Man had run so fast, he had left everyone far behind.

On and on ran the Gingerbread man. After a little while he came to a farm. Standing by the gate were two fat little piglets looking very forlorn.

"The farmer is late with our dinner," moaned one little piglet.

"And we are both very hungry," groaned the other one.

Then they began to squeal at the top of their voices. "We want our dinner! We want our dinner!"

Suddenly both little piglets stopped and looked at the Gingerbread Man. "Dinner!" they squealed, and began to chase after him.

But the Gingerbread Man didn't care one little bit.

"An old man, an old woman, a little boy, a snappy spotted dog and three mowers can't catch me," boasted the Gingerbread Man, "and you two fat little piglets never will!" Then off he ran.

The two little piglets trotted back to the farm to find some dinner.

"He'll get gobbled up one fine day!" said one of the piglets.

"Hope so!" said the other.

As the Gingerbread Man hurried on, he crossed a meadow where a pony was grazing. When the pony noticed the Gingerbread Man, he trotted across.

"Where are you going in such a hurry?" asked the pony.

"An old man, an old woman, a little boy and a snappy spotted dog are all trying to catch me," laughed the Gingerbread Man. "But I'm far too fast for them!"

Now the pony liked to eat grass and carrots and hay, but he loved to eat sweet crunchy biscuits even more.

"If they can't catch you, I will, and I'll gobble you up in a couple of bites!" said the pony and he began to chase the Gingerbread Man round and round the meadow.

But try as he might, the pony couldn't keep up with the speedy Gingerbread Man.

"Run! Run! As fast as you can! You can't catch me, I'm the Gingerbread Man!" Then he ran out of the meadow and scrambled up onto a river bank.

The Gingerbread Man gazed down in dismay, the river was wide and the water looked deep.

"Oh dear me!" the Gingerbread Man sighed. "Very soon, the old man, the old woman, the little boy, the snappy spotted dog and the pony will catch up with me...and I can't swim."

Now the Gingerbread Man hadn't noticed a sly red fox hiding in the reeds by the river.

"My dear Gingerbread Man," called the fox, trying very hard not to lick his lips. "Are you in some kind of trouble?"

"I'm in a bit of a hurry," replied the Gingerbread Man. "I need to cross the river as quick as possible, and I'm afraid I can't swim!"

"No problem," smiled the crafty fox. "I happen to be a very strong swimmer. Jump onto my back and I will carry you across with pleasure."

When they reached the middle of the river, the fox asked the Gingerbread Man to climb onto his head, just in case he got wet.

"My dear Gingerbread Man," called the fox as he swam along. "The water is getting much deeper now. I'm afraid you might drown."

"What shall I do?" the poor Gingerbread Man wailed.

"Could you possibly climb onto my nose?" asked the sly old fox.

As soon as he did, the fox tossed him up into the air, opened his mouth wide, and gobbled up the Gingerbread Man in one bite!

And that was the end of him.

Nobody could catch the Gingerbread Man, not the old man, or the old woman, or the little boy, or the snappy spotted dog, or the three mowers, or the hungry little piglets or the pony.

But the clever old fox did, didn't he?

The End

Little Red Riding Hood

There was once a little girl who lived with her parents in a cottage on the edge of a large forest.

Her father was a woodcutter, and each morning he would go deep into the forest where he worked hard all day long chopping down trees.

For her birthday one year, the little girl's grandmother made her a red cloak with a hood to match. The little girl wore her beautiful cloak every time she went outside – and that is why she became known as Little Red Riding Hood.

One day when Little Red Riding Hood was playing in the garden, she heard her mother calling from the cottage.

"Your grandmother is not very well, and she has decided to stay in bed today. Perhaps you could take her something to cheer her up."

So together they packed a basket. They put in a freshly baked loaf of bread, some butter and a jar of strawberry jam.

Then Little Red Riding Hood laid a clean cloth on top of the basket, and she was ready to go to her grandmother's house.

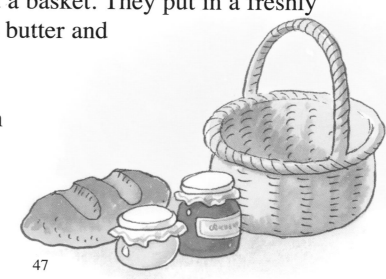

Now Little Red Riding Hood's grandmother lived on the other side of the forest. So before she set off, her mother made the little girl promise never to stray from the path, and never to talk to strangers.

Little Red Riding Hood listened carefully, then off she went dressed in her special red cloak.

"Go straight to Grandmother's house, and remember to keep to the path!" her mother called as she watched her disappear into the forest.

Red Riding Hood was half way to her grandmother's house when a big grey wolf stepped out from behind a tree.

"Good morning, my dear. What a simply lovely red cloak you have on!" said the wolf, doing his best to look friendly.

When Little Red Riding Hood heard this, she forgot what her mother had told her, and she began to talk to the wolf.

"My grandmother made it for my birthday," said the little girl politely. "She is ill in bed now, and I am going to cheer her up!"

"How very kind, my dear," smiled the wolf trying not to show his sharp teeth.

"And what have you got in your basket for Grandmother?" the wolf asked Little Red Riding Hood.

"Freshly baked bread, golden butter and her favourite strawberry jam," she replied.

"How simply delicious," said the wolf licking his lips.

Can you believe that at that very moment, the wicked wolf was planning to gobble up Little Red Riding Hood, and her grandmother too, if he had half a chance!

"Where does your grandmother live?" asked the wicked wolf.

"Right at the end of this path on the far side of the forest," said Little Red Riding Hood as she walked along.

"Why not take some of these beautiful flowers to your grandmother?" suggested the wolf – for he was trying to delay Little Red Riding Hood as long as he could.

When the little girl saw the flowers growing by the path, she stopped at once and began to pick them.

Red Riding Hood was so busy, she never noticed the wolf bound off down the path towards her grandmother's house.

Perhaps the wolf knew a short cut through the trees, for in less time than it takes to tell, he was knocking on Grandmother's door.

"Who is it?" called the old lady from her bed.

"It's Little Red Riding Hood," whispered the wolf as softly as he could.

"Just lift up the latch and walk right in!" said the grandmother.

The big grey wolf rushed through the door, bounded into the bedroom and leapt onto Grandmother's bed.

When the poor old lady heard the wolf snarl, and saw his sharp pointed teeth, she threw back the bedclothes, jumped out of bed, ran outside and hid behind the woodshed.

Meanwhile, the wolf put on one of Grandmother's spare nightdresses and one of her frilly nightcaps. He even found a spare pair of glasses on a table by the bed.

"I feel these glasses suit me very well. I really do look like a grandmother!" and the wolf smiled as he admired himself in the mirror.

"When Little Red Riding Hood arrives, I shall gobble her up, and I'll eat her grandmother later!" and the wolf sniggered and snapped his teeth loudly.

Then he jumped into Grandmother's bed, and pulled the bedclothes up to his eyes.

Before very long, Little Red Riding Hood came skipping up the path and knocked gently on her grandmother's door.

"Who is there?" croaked the wolf trying his best to sound like the old lady.

"It's Little Red Riding Hood, come to cheer you up," the little girl replied.

"Just lift the latch and walk right in!" said the wolf.

"How strange Grandmother sounds, perhaps she has a sore throat," Little Red Riding Hood thought to herself.

"How are you feeling today?" the little girl asked as she tiptoed across her grandmother's room. But when the little girl put down her basket and flowers, she jumped back in surprise.

"Why Grandmother, what big ears you have!" she cried.

"All the better to hear you with!" said the wolf in a deep voice. "Come closer my dear!"

So Little Red Riding Hood stepped a little closer to her grandmother's bed.

"Why Grandmother, what big eyes you have!" said the little girl staring at the wolf in her grandmother's silver glasses.

"All the better to see you with!" grinned the wolf. "Come closer my dear!"

So Little Red Riding Hood took one more step forward, and looked very carefully at the wolf in her grandmother's nightdress and frilly nightcap.

"Why Grandmother, what big teeth you have!" gasped Little Red Riding Hood.

"All the better to EAT you with!" snarled the wolf as he leapt out of bed.

"You're not my grandmother!" yelled Little Red Riding Hood.

"Indeed I'm not," growled the wolf. "I'm the big bad wolf, and I'm going to gobble you up!"

When she heard that, Little Red Riding Hood ran out of the room screaming at the top of her voice, with the wolf close behind her.

As she rushed out of the front door, she fell right into the arms of her father, the woodcutter.

He had been chopping down trees nearby, along with some of the other woodsmen. When he heard Little Red Riding Hood's screams, and saw Grandmother peeping from behind the woodshed, he guessed that something was wrong.

"The wolf is going to gobble me up," shrieked the little girl. "Look! He's right behind me!"

When the woodcutter saw the wolf running out of Grandmother's front door, he grabbed his sharp axe, ready to chop off the wolf's head.

When the wolf saw the woodcutter, he trembled with fright, and ran for his life.

"That wicked wolf must have gobbled up poor Grandmother," sobbed Little Red Riding Hood.

"No he hasn't!" smiled the little girl's father. "There she is. She's been hiding behind the woodshed all the time."

How happy everyone felt. Grandmother was safe, and feeling much better in spite of her fright. Little Red Riding Hood was safe too, thanks to her brave father.

The wicked wolf was gone forever, and would never
return while the woodcutters were in the forest.

It was getting late so the woodcutters headed for home.
No doubt they would tell their children that night, how they
had chased a big bad wolf, who was dressed in a nightdress
and frilly nightcap!

The End

The Ugly Duckling

It was a warm day in summer, and a mother duck was sitting all by herself on her nest at the far end of a pond. She felt rather lonely, for it seemed to her that she'd been there for ever.

At long last one of the eggs cracked open, and out popped a tiny duckling, then another and another. Before very long, there were six fluffy yellow ducklings doing their best to jump out of the nest.

Then she noticed that the biggest of her eggs hadn't hatched. So she settled down to keep the egg warm underneath her soft feathers.

While the mother duck waited, she watched her ducklings scurrying to and fro as they explored their new world.

"I do believe that the world is a great deal bigger than our pond," she quacked, nodding her head wisely. "It stretches right up to the farmyard...and that's as far as it goes I think!"

It didn't take long before the big egg began to crack
open, and a large grey bird with a huge head and a
long neck came tumbling out of its shell.

"Oh my! Oh my!" quacked the mother duck.

"You don't look a bit like your brothers and sisters.
I'm not even sure that you are a duckling at all!"

As soon as the other six ducklings heard all the noise,
they scurried out of the reeds and gathered round the new
arrival.

"Oh my!" said the mother duck with a sigh. "He does look rather funny, a bit strange, you might say."

"He's not like us!" cheeped the smallest of the six ducklings. Then the others joined in. "He's not even yellow!" "His head is too big!" "His feet are enormous!"

"His neck is long and skinny!" "AND HE'S UGLY!"

"Now, that is not so," said the mother duck. "He's not ugly, he's just different!"

But sad to say, from that day on, the poor duckling became known as the Ugly Duckling.

Mother duck was eager to show off her newly hatched family, so she led them down to the pond for their first swim.

When they reached the water's edge, the ducklings plopped in one by one, and soon they were swimming round in the water.

"Don't you dare come near us!" the six yellow ducklings shouted to the Ugly Duckling as they bobbed up and down near their mother.

"Why, he's the best swimmer of you all!" quacked the mother duck. "He may look different, but one day, he'll outshine every one of you!"

After a while, the mother duck led her ducklings across the pond and into the farmyard.

The geese and the rest of the birds gathered round and stared when they saw the Ugly Duckling.

"What is that?" hissed the farmyard gander rudely.

"He's the biggest of my new ducklings," the mother duck replied.

"He's the ugliest!" crowed the cockerel at the top of his voice.

The Ugly Duckling's six brothers and sisters cheeped with laughter, and the rest of the farmyard birds joined in.

Everyone was so unkind, it made the poor Ugly Duckling feel very unhappy.

As the weeks went by, the ducklings and their mother spent more and more time in the farmyard. The Ugly Duckling was pecked and hassled all day long.

"They tease me because I'm so ugly," thought the Ugly Duckling as he tried to get away from the other birds.

One morning a girl from the farmhouse came into the yard to feed the poultry.

"Get out of my way, you ugly creature!" and she threw grain from her bucket at the Ugly Duckling.

The duckling was so shocked, he tumbled through the hedge, and landed upside-down in a field full of sharp corn stalks.

The sparrows and finches that were perching on the branches fluttered up into the sky with fright.

"Everyone I meet is frightened of me because of the way I look," sighed the Ugly Duckling. "It must be because I am so ugly. I shall go far away from here and never come back again!"

So early next morning, he ran away from the cruel birds in the farmyard.

The Ugly Duckling travelled all day long. At last he came to a great open marsh where the wild ducks lived.

"You're not the prettiest of ducks!" quacked one of the drakes. "But you're welcome to stay here as long as you like," and away he flew.

Week after week the Ugly Duckling hid in the rushes all alone. Nobody bothered him, until one day, a hunting dog came sniffing round.

The wild ducks flew off at once. There were men on the marsh carrying guns, and the wild ducks knew not to stay.

When the hunting dog discovered the Ugly Duckling, he growled and bared his teeth, then he turned and ran off into the reeds.

"Even the dog thinks I'm ugly," said the duckling. "That is the reason he didn't bite me!"

It was autumn now, and the weather was getting colder day by day. It was time for the Ugly Duckling to leave the marsh and find somewhere away from the wind and the rain.

After a long search, he came upon a tumbledown cottage. It looked quite empty, so the duckling squeezed through a hole in the door where the wood had rotted away.

Once inside the cottage, he hid in a corner and fell fast asleep.

When the Ugly Duckling woke up the next morning, he was in for quite a surprise. An old woman lived there with her cat and her hen and she found the duckling as soon as it was light.

The old woman was delighted the duckling had come and she begged him to stay. She thought he would lay plenty of duck eggs for tea.

But her companions, the cat and the hen, had other ideas.

"I can catch mice! Can you?" snarled the cat.

The Ugly Duckling shook his head.

"I can lay eggs! Can you?" clucked the hen.

The Ugly Duckling shook his head again, for he had no idea how to lay an egg.

"The old woman will fatten you up and eat you for dinner, you ugly bird!" sneered the cat and the hen.

Their bullying went on and on and on. So after a while, although winter had arrived, the Ugly Duckling knew he had to move on.

So early one morning, before anyone in the cottage was awake, he squeezed out of the door where the wood had rotted away.

As the duckling walked through the day, snowflakes began to fall. Then, at long last, he came to a quiet lake. And there he stayed all alone. By day he swam in the icy water, and when darkness fell he went to sleep in the hollow of an old tree.

One evening as the sun was setting, and a mist was drifting across the lake, the Ugly Duckling looked up and saw a flock of beautiful birds passing overhead.

"How I wish I was one of those birds, then I could fly away with them and be happy for ever."

That night he stayed on the water dreaming of those wonderful birds. But by morning the lake had turned to ice. The poor duckling was frozen fast and couldn't move.

A farmer, who happened to be passing by, freed the poor bird and carried him home in his thick jacket.

The farmhouse kitchen was cosy and warm, and the Ugly Duckling soon thawed out. The farmer's children were very young and wanted to play with him. It seemed like fun to them.

But the Ugly Duckling didn't know they were just being friendly; he was frightened and tried to get away.

He stumbled around the kitchen in panic, he knocked over the milk, fell into the flour and then ran across the butter.

The farmer's wife clapped her hands, the children screamed and the farmer chased him out of the door!

So the Ugly Duckling fled to the lake, and went back and hid in the hollow tree. He stayed there until the snow was gone and the ice had melted away.

Spring came at last! The weather was warm and sunny, and great flocks of birds returned to the lake. Winter was gone, and for the first time in his life the Ugly Duckling felt happy to be alive.

Boldly he swam into the middle of the lake, then he spread out his strong wings and soared high into the air...he could fly!

As he landed gracefully at the edge of the lake, he saw his reflection in the clear water. Looking back at him was a beautiful white bird.

He could hardly believe his eyes, for during the long months of winter, the Ugly Duckling had grown into a magnificent swan.

Very soon, the other swans on the lake came gliding across the water to make him welcome.

"Are you on your own?" asked one of the swans in the kindest way.

"Please come and live with us," said another.

No words can ever describe how happy this made the beautiful new swan feel.

The new swan's dreams had come true at last, and no one would ever call him ugly again.

The End

Alice in Wonderland

Alice was beginning to get very tired of sitting by her sister on a grassy bank, and of having nothing to do. The hot day was making her feel very sleepy.

Then, just when she was wondering if she should make a daisy chain, a White Rabbit with pink eyes ran close by her.

There was nothing so very remarkable in that, nor did Alice find it strange when she heard the White Rabbit say to himself, "Oh dear! I shall be late!"

But when the White Rabbit took a watch out of his waistcoat pocket, looked at it and then hurried on, Alice jumped to her feet. For it flashed across her mind that she had never seen a rabbit in a waistcoat holding a watch!

Burning with curiosity, Alice ran across the field after him and saw him hurry down a large rabbit-hole under the hedge.

In another moment down went Alice after the White Rabbit, never once thinking how she was going to get out again.

The rabbit-hole went straight on like a tunnel for some time, then dipped down suddenly, and Alice found herself falling down a very deep well.

Either the well was very deep, or she fell very slowly, for Alice had plenty of time to look around as she floated downwards.

The sides of the well were filled with cupboards and book-shelves, and here and there she saw maps and pictures hanging on pegs.

Down, down, down she went. Would the fall ever come to an end? Then suddenly, thump, thump, thump! Down she came on a heap of sticks and dry leaves, and the fall was over.

Alice was not hurt a bit and jumped to her feet in a moment. In front of her stretched a long passage; luckily the White Rabbit was still in sight.

Alice sped after him and was just in time to hear him say, "Oh my ears and whiskers, how late it's getting!"

He turned the corner and was gone, and Alice found herself in a long low hall.

There were doors all round the hall. Alice tried every one, but they were all locked. Suddenly she saw a glass table and on the top was a tiny golden key – but it was far too small to open any of the doors.

However, Alice took a second look and spied a low curtain she had not noticed before. Behind it was a small door, which was as high as her knee. To her delight the little golden key fit perfectly, and when Alice knelt down to look straight through the door, she discovered the most beautiful garden you could ever imagine.

But there seemed no reason at all to wait by the small door, for Alice couldn't even push her head through the doorway, so she went back to the glass table.

This time she found a bottle that had not been there before. Round the neck of the bottle was a label marked DRINK ME.

Alice took a sip of the mixture. It tasted so delicious, she drank the lot!

"What a curious feeling!" said Alice as she grew smaller and smaller. "I must be shutting up like a telescope."

Now she was just the right size to go through the small doorway into the beautiful garden.

But alas for poor Alice, she had left the little golden key on top of the glass table, and now she could not possibly reach it.

She tried her best to climb up one of the table-legs, but it was far too slippery. Poor Alice sat down and cried.

It was then she noticed a glass box underneath the table. In it was a small cake with the words EAT ME marked on top in currants.

"Well, I'll eat it," said Alice, "and if it makes me grow larger, I can reach the key, and if it makes me grow smaller, I can creep under the door and get into the beautiful garden."

As soon as Alice finished the cake, she grew so large she bumped her head on the ceiling. Poor Alice burst into floods of tears. Now she could only see into the garden with one eye.

She cried so much that a large pool of her tears reached halfway down the hall.

After a while she heard a pattering of feet in the distance. It was the White Rabbit. He got such a fright when he saw the giant Alice, he dropped the fan and gloves he was carrying and scurried away.

Alice picked them up, and as the hall was very hot, she began to fan herself. How strange and muddled she felt sitting all alone in a pool of her own tears.

As she looked down at her hands, Alice was surprised to see that she had put on one of the White Rabbit's little gloves, and it fit perfectly.

"How can I have done that?" she thought. Alice was shrinking rapidly and soon realised it must be the fan, so she dropped it at once.

She was now small enough to go through the door into the beautiful garden at last. But unfortunately the door was locked, and the tiny golden key was back on top of the glass table.

"Things are worse than ever now," sobbed Alice. "I was never as small as this before!"

As she spoke these words, her foot slipped and she was up to her neck in salt water. At first she thought she had fallen into the sea, but she soon realised she had fallen into a pool of her own tears which she had cried when she was huge.

"I wish I hadn't cried so much," said Alice as she swam about.

Then she heard something splashing about in the pool a little way off. At first she thought it was a walrus or a hippopotamus, but when she remembered how small she was, she realised it was only a mouse that had fallen in just like herself.

While Alice was talking to the Mouse and trying to get to know him, several other peculiar creatures joined them in the pool of tears.

Alice thought it was high time to go, so she led the way, and the whole party swam to the shore.

An odd-looking Dodo bird held races on the sand, and soon all the creatures were dry.

"Everyone has won, and all must have prizes," said the Dodo bird when the races were finished.

Alice put her hand in her pocket and pulled out a box of sweets, (luckily the salt water had not got into it). She handed them round as prizes, and there was exactly one each.

Later on, when Alice began to tell the peculiar creatures about her cat (who caught mice and birds), every one of them hurried away. Alice was left all alone, so she set off to find someone else to talk to.

A great question began to puzzle Alice as she looked at the tall blades of grass around her. "How can I manage to grow big again? I ought to eat or drink something!"

A large mushroom was growing nearby, so she peered over the edge and found herself staring at a blue caterpillar smoking a hookah pipe.

"Who are you?" enquired the Caterpillar sleepily.

"I hardly know!" said Alice. "Being so many different sizes in one day is very confusing!"

"What size do you want to be?" asked the Caterpillar.

"A little larger than I am now," replied Alice (as she was almost the same size as the caterpillar).

"You're a very good height indeed," muttered the Caterpillar as he crawled away. "One side of the mushroom will make you taller, the other side shorter!"

Quickly Alice broke off a piece from either side. When she nibbled the piece in her left hand, she grew taller than the tops of the trees. And when she bit into the piece in her right hand she shrank down a bit.

As she walked through the woods deciding what to do next, Alice came upon a very small house.

"Anyone who lives here will be frightened out of their wits if they see me this size," thought Alice. So she nibbled the right-hand side of the mushroom until she was small enough to go up to the door.

But when she heard the howling, sneezing and crashing noises that were coming from inside, Alice didn't bother to knock, there was no point!

She pushed open a door that led into a kitchen full of smoke from end to end. A duchess was sitting on a stool nursing a baby, and a cook was leaning over the fire shaking a pepper pot into a pan of soup.

The air was so full of pepper it made Alice sneeze, and the poor baby howled and sneezed without a pause.

A large cat was sitting on the hearth grinning from ear to ear. "Please would you tell me," said Alice, "why your cat grins like that?"

"It's a Cheshire Cat, that's why, Pig!" Alice was quite startled for she thought the Duchess meant her...but it was her baby she was speaking to.

All of a sudden the cook took the pan of soup off the fire and began throwing fire-irons, plates and dishes at the Duchess and the baby.

Alice was really alarmed when the Duchess started to sing a lullaby; at the end of each line she tossed the poor baby up and down until it howled.

"Here! You may nurse it a bit, if you like!" called the Duchess as she flung her baby at Alice. "I must go and get ready to play croquet with the Queen."

Alice caught the wriggling baby and took it outside, and when it began to snort and grunt, Alice looked at its face and found it had turned into a PIG!

So she put the little creature down and it trotted away quietly into the wood.

Alice was suddenly shocked to see the Cheshire Cat sitting grinning on the bough of a tree a little way off.

"Cheshire Puss," she began, "could you tell me, please, which way I ought to go from here?"

"In that direction," said the Cat waving his right paw, "lives a Hatter, and in that direction," waving the other paw, "lives a March Hare. Visit either of them, they're both mad!"

And with that the Cheshire Cat disappeared quite slowly, beginning with his tail and ending with his grin.

Before too long, Alice came to the March Hare's house. It was the right place because the chimneys were shaped like ears and the roof was thatched with fur.

A table was set out in the front of the house, and the March Hare and the Hatter were seated at one corner having tea. A dormouse was sitting between them fast asleep, and the other two were using him as a cushion.

"No room! No room!" they cried when they saw Alice coming.

"There's plenty of room!" said Alice indignantly, and she sat down in an armchair at one end of the table.

"What day is it?" the Hatter said to Alice shaking his watch and holding it to his ear.

"The fourth," Alice replied.

"Two days wrong," sighed the Hatter. "I told you butter wouldn't suit the works!" he added, looking angrily at the March Hare.

"It was the best butter," the March Hare meekly replied, then he took the watch and dipped it into his tea.

The March Hare suggested that Alice
should tell them a story.

"I'm afraid I don't know one," said Alice.

"Then the Dormouse shall!" they both
cried, and pinched him on both sides at once.

The Dormouse opened his eyes and began to
tell his tale, but the other two kept moving places and
interrupting so often, Alice got up and walked off in disgust.

The Dormouse fell asleep at once, and when Alice looked back,
the March Hare and the Hatter had put him in the teapot!

As she went through the wood Alice noticed a door in one of the
tree trunks...so she went in. Once more she found herself in the long
hall close to the glass table.

"I won't make the same mistake this time," thought Alice and took
the golden key and unlocked the small door. Quickly she nibbled a
piece of the mushroom that she had kept in her pocket. And when
she was small enough, she went through the door straight into the
beautiful garden.

A large rose-tree stood near the entrance of the garden. The roses growing on it were white, but three gardeners with bodies like playing cards were busy painting the roses red. Alice was curious to know why.

"Why Miss, this ought to be a red rose, and if the Queen finds out she will have our heads cut off!"

At that moment one of the gardeners called out, "The Queen! The Queen!" and all three began to tremble with fear. The Queen and King of Hearts were approaching. When they reached Alice they stopped and looked at her.

The Queen demanded to know Alice's name. Then she saw the trembling gardeners.

"Off with their heads!" she screamed when she saw the roses covered in red paint.

But the moment the royal party moved off, Alice popped the poor gardeners into a large flowerpot to keep them safe.

"Do you play croquet?" shouted the Queen when she noticed Alice again, and when Alice replied that she did, the strangest game began...the balls were live hedgehogs, the mallets live flamingoes, and the soldiers, (who were really cards) had to double themselves up to make the arches.

Alice found it almost impossible to control her flamingo, and the hedgehogs kept unrolling themselves and scampering away.

None of the players waited their turn, they quarrelled all the time and fought over the hedgehogs. In a very short time the Queen was in a furious temper and kept shouting, "Off with his head!" or "Off with her head!" about once a minute.

Alice began to feel very uneasy. "They're very fond of beheading people here. It's amazing there's anyone left alive!"

As she was wondering how she might escape without being seen, a curious face appeared in the air. It was the Chesire Cat.

At least now Alice would have someone to talk to.

"How do you like the Queen?" whispered the Cat.

"Not at all," said Alice, but before she could finish her sentence the King came by.

"I don't like the look of it at all," said the King looking at the Cat's head with great curiosity, and he called to the Queen to remove it.

The Queen had only one way of settling this and called for the executioner. But how can you cut off a head unless it's attached to a body? And before anyone had time to decide, the Cat's head faded slowly and was gone.

In the distance a cry was heard, "The trial is beginning!"

"What trial is that?" panted Alice as she ran to join in with the rest of the crowd.

The King and Queen of Hearts were seated
on their thrones when Alice arrived in court.

The Knave of Hearts was standing in front of
them in chains, and a large dish of tarts was on
a table. In the jury box were twelve creatures
all writing busily on slates.

"Herald, read the accusation!" said the King.
At this, the White Rabbit blew three blasts
on his trumpet and unrolled a scroll.

*"The Queen of Hearts she made some tarts,
All on a summer day:
The Knave of Hearts he stole those tarts,
And took them quite away."*

The first witness called was the Hatter. As he
gave his evidence, Alice realised she was beginning to grow larger.

Can you imagine her surprise when the White Rabbit called Alice as a witness!

Forgetting she was getting bigger by the minute, Alice jumped up and knocked over the jury box.

At this moment the King called out "Silence! All persons more than a mile high must leave the court!"

"Stuff and nonsense!" said Alice loudly.

"Off with her head!" the Queen shouted at the top of her voice.

"You're nothing but a pack of cards!" said Alice (who had grown to full size by now).

At this the whole pack rose up into the air and came flying down on her. Alice gave a little scream and tried to beat them off.

Then Alice heard a faraway voice calling her name, and she found herself lying on the grassy bank, by her sister, who was gently brushing away some leaves that had fallen onto her face.

"Wake up, Alice!" said her sister. "Why, what a long sleep you've had!"

"I've had such a curious dream!" said Alice, and she told her sister all the strange adventures you have just been reading about.

The End

The Adventures of Pinocchio

Once upon a time a woodcutter was chopping a log of wood when suddenly he heard a voice crying, "Stop hitting me you cruel fellow!" The words seemed to come from the log.

The poor man was terrified and ran to find Geppetto the toymaker.

"Oh please take this piece of wood and burn it," begged the woodcutter, trembling from head to toe. "I swear it spoke to me!"

Geppetto was delighted as soon as he heard this and had no intention of throwing the log on the fire.

"I'm going to make myself a puppet that looks like a real boy, and this strange log is perfect," Geppetto decided.

So straight away he turned back to his workbench and began to carve the wood.

"I shall call my puppet Pinocchio and he will be the son I have always dreamed of."

Poor Geppetto was in for a big surprise! As soon as he had carved Pinocchio's head, the naughty puppet stuck out his tongue.

"You rude boy," scolded Geppetto. "Have you no respect for your father?"

Worse was to come. The second his legs were finished, Pinocchio kicked Geppetto hard then raced out of the door.

"Come back home you wicked boy!" yelled Geppetto, shaking his fist angrily as he chased after his puppet.

"What's all this commotion?" hollered a stern-looking policeman when Pinocchio leapt into his arms.

"He's trying to run away from me, give him back at once!" shouted Geppetto, still very angry.

"Don't you tell me what to do!" snapped the policeman and he marched Geppetto off to jail.

Before too long he realized that Geppetto was a kind old man who meant no harm, so he apologized for locking him up and let him go.

Sadly Geppetto made his way back home. "I doubt if I will ever see my Pinocchio again," he sighed.

"I'm so pleased you're back, father," cried a voice the moment Geppetto opened the door. "I'll be a good boy from now on and never run away again!"

At first Geppetto thought it must be a child who lived nearby, but no, it was his own little Pinocchio.

"You can speak just like a real boy," gasped Geppetto and his eyes filled with tears of joy.

That night the old man made Pinocchio some smart new clothes. "Tomorrow you must go to school and learn to read and write as all good boys do."

"I can't go to school without a reading book," gasped
Pinocchio the next morning. So although it was bitterly cold,
Geppetto rushed outside and sold his only coat to buy a book.

"Thank you, dear father," said Pinocchio as he kissed the old
man goodbye. "I promise I will go to school every day and make
you proud."

As Pinocchio hurried down the cobbled street he heard music
playing. He turned the corner, and there in the middle of the town
square was a travelling theatre.

"Buy a ticket to see *The Great Puppet Show*!" a boy banging
on a drum was shouting.

In an instant Pinocchio forgot all about school and his promise to Geppetto. He sold his reading book for two pennies and bought a ticket to the show.

When Pinocchio saw the puppets singing and dancing he simply had to join in.

At first Enrico, the theatre manager, was extremely angry and tried to throw Pinocchio off the stage, but when the audience started to shower this amazing new puppet with gold coins, he quickly changed his mind!

All that day Pinocchio performed with the other puppets until the theatre closed.

"I've never taken so much money," chuckled Enrico as he handed Pinocchio five gold coins. "Go home to your father, you clever little puppet, and tell him to buy himself a new coat!"

Now Pinocchio did intend to go straight home, but on the way he met a cat pretending to be blind and a fox pretending to be lame. This rascally pair were really two cunning thieves looking for someone to rob.

"Do you want to know how to make your money grow?" asked the cat when he spied Pinocchio's five gold coins.

"We know a place called Miracle Meadow," the fox said. "If you bury your coins there, a tree will grow covered in money."

"Do tell me where it is," pleaded Pinocchio. Then the scheming pair drew closer and whispered in his ear – and the silly puppet believed every word they said.

Off went the cat and the fox at top speed, and as you may have guessed, Pinocchio set off to find the Miracle Meadow and make his fortune.

On the way there a couple of ghostly figures tried to rob him…it was the cat and the fox in disguise of course!

However, Pinocchio was crafty and hid his coins under his tongue. The two thieves were so angry when they failed to find the money, they tied him to a tree and went off empty-handed.

Poor Pinocchio felt so alone and afraid, how he longed to be back home with Geppetto.

Luckily his fortunes were about to change. The Blue Fairy, who helped people in trouble, noticed Pinocchio's plight. She clapped her hands twice and an owl flew down from a tree.

"Untie that unfortunate puppet and bring him to me!" she commanded.

When Pinocchio saw the Blue Fairy, he cheered up at once. Quickly he told her what had happened…but he didn't tell the truth.

As he spoke something extraordinary happened. His nose began to grow! The more lies he told, the longer his nose became.

"Why were you tied to a tree and where is your money?" enquired the Blue Fairy.

"Bandits kidnapped me on my way home, they took my reading book and stole my five coins," lied Pinocchio. By now his nose was ENORMOUS!

"Tell one more lie and your nose will be longer than a broomstick," warned the Blue Fairy, for she knew none of this had happened and the coins were in his pocket.

"Do what I ask," the Blue Fairy spoke kindly, "then one day I will grant you your dearest wish."

"I want to be a real boy, please!" cried Pinocchio.

"Go home to Geppetto, work hard at school, be truthful and kind and your wish will be granted," promised the Blue Fairy.

Maybe you thought Pinocchio was so grateful to the Blue Fairy that he ran straight home...he did nothing of the kind!

Walking back through Miracle Meadow, he simply couldn't resist burying his coins and waiting for them to grow. Needless to say, the crafty cat and fox were lying in wait, ready to steal his money and run away!

When at last Pinocchio returned home, Geppetto was overjoyed and gladly forgave him. For a short while, Pinocchio kept the promise he had made. He was truthful and kind, he went to school every single day and learned to read and write.

Unfortunately this was all due
to change when he made friends
with Tito, the naughtiest, laziest
boy in the class.

One day, Tito told Pinocchio
about a place called Toyland.
"There's no school, and instead
of doing dull lessons, everyone
lazes around all day," giggled Tito.
"A coach leaves at midnight, let's get on it!"

Pinocchio could hardly wait, and late that night as the coach
passed through town, both of them climbed aboard.

Strangely the coach looked more like a cage. So many boys
were crammed inside, some had to ride on top.

Stranger still, all the donkeys pulling the coach wore boots
of white leather tied with laces!

Once in Toyland, Pinocchio and Tito had the time of their lives. No school, no lessons and no teachers…what could be better?

Oddly, none of the boys who arrived on the coach wondered why they had been brought to this place. Before very long they would find out!

As he wandered round Toyland one morning Pinocchio saw, to his horror, that most of the boys had grown long furry ears.

"We're all turning into donkeys!" shrieked Tito.

And when Pinocchio raised his hands to his ears, he screamed with fright too.

"Look! I've grown a tail!" Tito gasped in horror.

"So have I!" said Pinocchio, and he began to bray like a donkey.

Sadly that was to be the fate of every naughty boy who had come to live in Toyland…they were turned into donkeys and sold.

Pinocchio was bought by a ringmaster and went to work in the circus. He was taught to jump through hoops, but when he stumbled in the ring and hurt his leg the ringmaster was furious.

"A lame donkey is no good to me. You must go to market and be sold!"

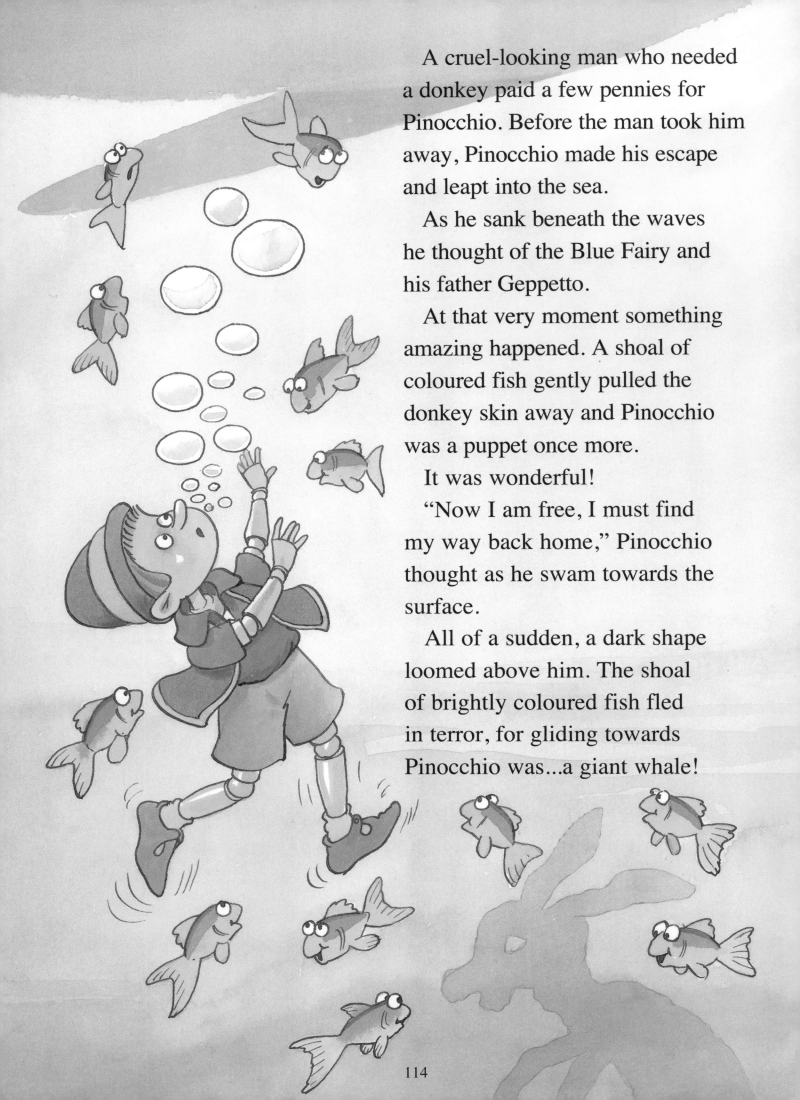

A cruel-looking man who needed a donkey paid a few pennies for Pinocchio. Before the man took him away, Pinocchio made his escape and leapt into the sea.

As he sank beneath the waves he thought of the Blue Fairy and his father Geppetto.

At that very moment something amazing happened. A shoal of coloured fish gently pulled the donkey skin away and Pinocchio was a puppet once more.

It was wonderful!

"Now I am free, I must find my way back home," Pinocchio thought as he swam towards the surface.

All of a sudden, a dark shape loomed above him. The shoal of brightly coloured fish fled in terror, for gliding towards Pinocchio was...a giant whale!

There was no escape, for as the whale opened his gigantic mouth, Pinocchio was sucked inside and carried down into its stomach.

When the frightened puppet scrambled to his feet he could not believe his eyes.

Inside the whale, rows of golden lights gleamed from the mast of a tiny boat, and a familiar figure was standing inside.

It was his own dear Geppetto alive and well! Pinocchio had never felt so happy.

"Oh how I longed for you to come home. When you never returned," Geppetto explained, "I spent all my days searching for you. There was no trace of you in the town, so I loaded up my boat and put to sea! The whale swallowed me and I've been trapped in here ever since."

"How brave of you, father," said Pinocchio and a big tear rolled down his cheek. "Now we must try to escape."

And escape they did! Showing great courage, Pinocchio managed to control the boat and steer it slowly and carefully out of the whale's stomach.

"We'll soon be free, father!" called Pinocchio boldly, and when the whale rose to the surface and opened his huge mouth, the little boat floated out into the open sea.

Before Geppetto and Pinocchio realised what was happening, a powerful wave washed them onto a sandy beach...and waiting for them was the Blue Fairy.

"Pinocchio," she said gently, "you have shown such love for Geppetto, you truly deserve your dearest wish."

The Blue Fairy clapped her hands twice and Pinocchio became a real boy at last.

And so it was, after many adventures, and the special magic of the Blue Fairy, Pinocchio was a puppet no more.

Geppetto found the son he had always longed for...and they both lived happily ever after.

The Princess and the Pea

Once upon a time, so the story goes, there lived a certain Prince who longed to be married.

"Remember one important thing," said the Queen rather grandly, "when you find a wife, she must be a *real* princess!"

The Prince looked surprised. "What if I fall in love with someone wonderful and she isn't a *real* princess?" he asked in dismay.

"That simply will not do!" snapped the Queen. "She has to be a *real* princess or nothing!"

The Prince glanced at the King who seemed to be shaking his head. "I'm afraid that's how it works when you are a prince," he said quietly.

The Queen, however, did not notice, she was far too busy searching for something in an old oak chest.

"Here it is!" she cried. "My list of suitable princesses in every surrounding kingdom!"

The King heaved a long sigh. The Queen, however, did not notice, she was far too busy reading the names on the roll of parchment.

"Visit every castle on this list and you will be sure to find a *real* princess. Remember, nothing less will do!" And these were the Queen's last words on the subject.

So without further delay, the Prince set off on his search for a bride.

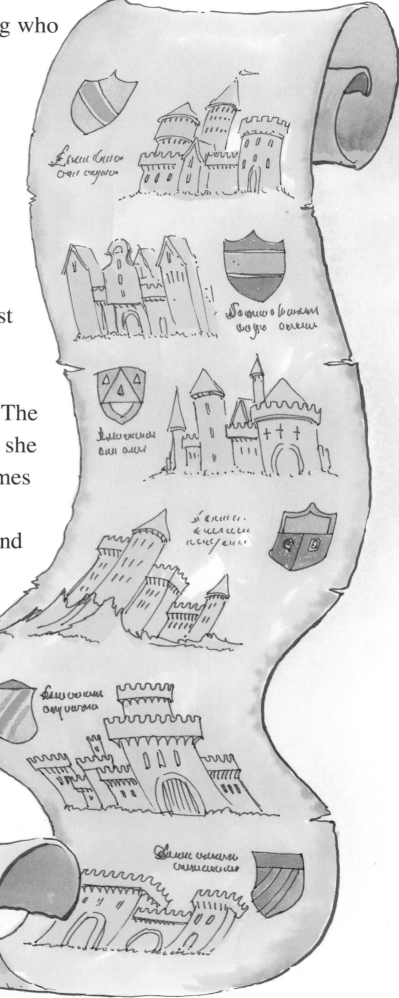

In the weeks that followed the Prince travelled far and visited many kingdoms. He made absolutely sure that he stopped at every castle on the Queen's list and he introduced himself to as many princesses as possible.

Before too long the Prince realised that his task was far from easy.

Some of the princesses seemed rather old, while others seemed far too young, and some of the castles were in ruins. This made the Prince wonder if the Queen's list was out of date.

There were some princesses, with absolutely no manners at all, who giggled and tittered the moment they saw him. It was very embarrassing.

He called on one princess who was so bad-tempered, she refused to open the castle door. Worse still, she pulled faces and yelled at him from the balcony!

Sadly the Prince lost all hope of ever finding a *real* princess he could marry. So feeling very tired and disappointed, he threw away the Queen's list and headed for home…now it so happened that right at the very bottom of the Queen's list was a magnificent castle which the Prince failed to see.

Could it be that the *real* princess he was seeking lived inside?

Now he may never know!

The Prince looked so sad when he returned to the castle alone, and the King tried his best to cheer him up.

"One day soon you will meet a princess that you really love, of that I am certain!" he assured him.

The Queen, on the other hand, remained quite firm.

"Tomorrow you must set off once more, and this time you have to try harder," she said crossly. "You can not expect a *real* princess to come knocking on the door!"

Later that night there was a terrible storm. Thunder shook the castle and lightning seemed to split the skies.

The Prince felt pleased to be back home safe and warm beside a blazing fire.

Then, above the sound of rain pouring and wind howling down the chimney, a knock was heard.

"Who could possibly be visiting us on such a wild night?" asked the Queen.

Straight away the King rose from his chair. "No need to summon the servants," he said, "I will go myself and see who is at the door."

To his amazement, the King found a beautiful young girl
in the doorway. The poor thing was shivering with cold, her
clothes were soaked and her shoes splattered with mud.

"Come inside at once, my dear!" The King had to shout
loudly to be heard above the noise of the gale.

Quickly he slammed the door, and then led the stranger into
the castle to warm herself by the fire.

And in that moment the Prince fell deeply in love with her.
At long last he had met the girl he wanted to marry.

"What brought you to the castle on a night like this?"
enquired the King.

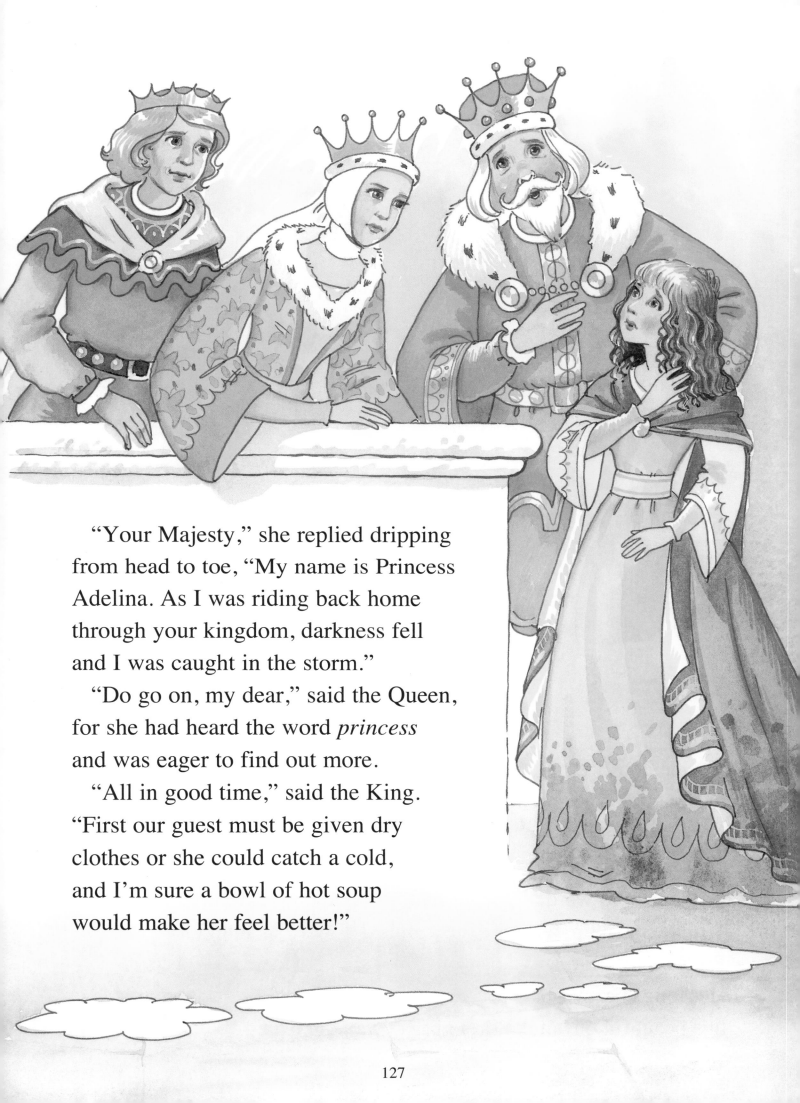

"Your Majesty," she replied dripping from head to toe, "My name is Princess Adelina. As I was riding back home through your kingdom, darkness fell and I was caught in the storm."

"Do go on, my dear," said the Queen, for she had heard the word *princess* and was eager to find out more.

"All in good time," said the King. "First our guest must be given dry clothes or she could catch a cold, and I'm sure a bowl of hot soup would make her feel better!"

"She doesn't look like a *real* princess to me," muttered the Queen under her breath, "but I know how to tell if she is genuine or not!"

So the Queen, determined as ever, rushed off to wake her servants who were already in bed at such a late hour.

In the meantime, a cosy fur-trimmed gown was found for the Princess to wear, and a pair of dainty slippers that fitted perfectly. Her long chestnut hair was dry now, and as the Prince gazed at this beautiful girl in the firelight, he was enchanted.

When she had finished supper, Princess Adelina told how her horse was startled by the thunder and had galloped off in the wrong direction.

"When I saw the lights shining from your castle windows, I rode up to the gates to find shelter," the Princess explained. "One of your grooms saw me and took my horse into the royal stables for the night."

And as the three sat comfortably by the fire, Princess Adelina listened spellbound to the King's stories about his kingdom, and the Prince fell more and more in love with her every minute.

Meanwhile, the Queen ordered her sleepy servants to make up a very special bed. "Bring me twenty of the firmest mattresses you can find!" she commanded.

The servants were bewildered at her strange request, but of course they obeyed.

Preparing the bed took ages, for the heavy mattresses had to be brought from every corner of the huge castle. Some of them were carried, some of them were pulled, while others were pushed and shoved.

"Place one on top of another," the Queen told her servants. Then when no one was looking, she popped a tiny dried pea under the first mattress.

"Now we shall see if Princess Adelina is a *real* princess or not!"

Before too long the pile of mattresses had grown so high, special steps were brought to reach up to the top.

"How truly splendid!" cried Princess Adelina when she saw her bed. "You should not have gone to all this effort for me!"

"No trouble at all," said the Queen as she watched the Princess climb up the steps. "Goodnight and sweet dreams, my dear."

"This bed looks so comfortable," Princess Adelina called down from the top of the twentieth mattress, "I shall fall asleep the moment my head touches the pillow!"

"We shall see," whispered the Queen as she closed the door.

During the night the terrible storm passed. The wind died down, the rain stopped, the thunder rolled away and all was peace and quiet.

Everyone in the castle was fast asleep except for Princess Adelina.

Her bed was so uncomfortable she tossed and turned all night long, and by morning she hadn't had a wink of sleep.

The poor girl was so tired, she could scarcely get out of bed and climb down the steps for breakfast.

"Did you sleep well, my dear?" the Queen asked eagerly the moment Princess Adelina came into the room.

"I'm afraid I did not," replied the Princess trying her best not to yawn.

The Queen held her breath.

"There was a small hard lump under my mattress," the Princess explained as she rubbed her sore back. "Perhaps it was a marble, or a bead, or a button that kept me awake all night."

"It was a pea!" cried the Queen with delight.

"A pea?" the King frowned.

"A pea?" the Prince gasped.

"A pea?" Princess Adelina looked puzzled.

"Yes, a tiny dried pea!" laughed the Queen. "Only a *real* princess would have a skin so tender that she could feel a tiny pea through twenty mattresses.

"I knew she was a *real* princess the second I met her!" cried the King joyfully.

"It never mattered to me," sighed the Prince as he gazed into Princess Adelina's eyes.

"I am so sorry I ever doubted you," said the Queen, and she threw her arms round the Princess and gave her a kiss.

"You were not to blame at all," Princess Adelina spoke to the Queen in the kindest way. "For who would expect a *real* princess to come knocking at the door on such a terrible night?"

Happily everything turned out well. The Prince asked the Princess if she would consent to be his bride, and she willingly agreed.

For as she told the King and Queen that morning, she had already fallen hopelessly in love with their son the moment she came in from the storm.

Later on, the Prince brought Princess Adelina her horse from the royal stable, and side by side they rode to her parents' kingdom.

"I must have visited every castle in my search for a bride! How could I have missed this one?" the Prince thought to himself as they came in sight of Princess Adelina's home.

Now as you may recall, this magnificent castle was right at the bottom of the Queen's list...*and the Prince had thrown it away!*

But thanks to a terrible storm and a tiny dried pea, this story has a perfect ending. The Prince and Princess married amid great rejoicing, and they lived happily ever after.

Princess Adelina made sure that the tiny dried pea was placed inside a special glass case, and there it remained for all to see.

And to this day, the story of the Princess and the Pea is often told in front of warm fires…especially on dark and stormy nights.

The End

The Adventures of Sinbad

Many years ago in an ancient eastern city there lived a young man whose name was Sinbad. His father, who was very rich, died and left his son a great deal of money. But in a short while Sinbad had foolishly wasted most of his father's wealth.

With what little money he had left, Sinbad decided to buy goods to trade in other lands. So he boarded a ship with several other merchants and put to sea.

"Our fortunes will be made on this voyage!" Sinbad called cheerfully to the men as the ship sailed out of the harbour.

Time went by and Sinbad's ship journeyed far across the ocean. Wherever it stopped, at ports or islands, people were eager to buy the merchant's goods in return for gold and silver, and Sinbad became a rich man once more.

One day, as the ship was passing a small island, the captain suggested that everyone might like to go ashore. Sinbad and the others had only been there for a short while when the whole island started to shudder and shake.

Suddenly, out of the water, rose the gigantic head of a sea monster! Fortunately the terrified men were thrown off its back before the monster dived beneath the waves.

The moment the captain thought everybody had returned safely to the ship he set sail, but in the confusion Sinbad was left behind clinging to a piece of wood.

And before that day was out, the swift current had taken him to the shores of another island.

Soon enough, Sinbad was discovered and taken before the King who ruled the island. The King was so impressed that Sinbad had managed to stay alive, he gave him a chest full of gold and a fast ship to carry him home.

Although Sinbad returned to his city a very rich man, he soon grew bored and longed for further adventures. Then one day a group of merchants asked Sinbad to join them on their next voyage.

All went well until they landed on a faraway desert island, where, by some strange chance, Sinbad was left behind once more. And when he gazed out to sea from the top of a palm tree, the ship was almost out of sight.

It was then he noticed a giant white ball near the beach, so he climbed down to investigate. Suddenly out of the sky a gigantic bird flew towards him. (He had often heard sailors tell of a fearsome bird called a Roc.)

As soon as the Roc sat down on its huge egg, Sinbad tied himself to the bird's leg with his turban, and when the Roc took off, Sinbad was carried away from the desert island.

The Roc flew high over the sea, and on reaching the mountains, it swooped down into a deep valley.

When the giant bird landed, Sinbad just managed to untie the knot of his turban before the Roc seized a serpent in its beak and flew away.

Sinbad looked about him and saw that the ground was covered in enormous diamonds, but coiled between the gems lay massive serpents dozing in the sun.

As he stood holding his sword in case the serpents awoke, something fell from the cliffs high above. When Sinbad glimpsed men standing on top of the cliffs, he quickly worked out what was happening.

They were hurling large pieces of meat onto the diamonds below, for they knew that the mountain eagles would fly down. The gems would stick to the meat, and then be carried back to the eagles' nests, where the men could collect them.

Now Sinbad knew of a way to escape! He picked up the biggest diamond and stuck it onto a piece of meat, and when the next eagle swooped down, he grabbed its legs and was carried out of the valley to safety.

And so it was, when Sinbad returned home, he was able to sell the magnificent diamond he had brought from the Valley of the Serpents and give the money to the poor in his city.

Sinbad had only been back for a while when he began to find life rather dull, so he chartered a ship and set sail once more.

After travelling for many days, the ship ran into a terrible storm. Very soon strong winds and towering waves drove it close to an island.

Before Sinbad and the other sailors could swim to the shore, hordes of savage creatures clambered up the sides of the ship and swarmed all over the deck.

Sinbad and the rest of the men were overpowered and dragged off to a castle on the island.

They were taken before a hideous giant with one bulging eye
that stared out of the middle of his forehead.

"Perhaps they will hold us for ransom or make us work as
slaves," whispered Sinbad.

That night they were locked up in prison, and next morning
were sent to work in the giant's forest. Seeing so many logs lying
on the ground gave Sinbad an idea!

In the days that followed, whenever the guards turned their
backs, the sailors built rafts that they managed to hide.

Late one night, when the guards had fallen asleep, Sinbad and
his friends made their escape from the castle. They hurried down
to the shore where the rafts were hidden, jumped aboard and
rowed quickly away from that awful island.

Most of the rafts were large and could carry several men. One raft was smaller than the rest, but it was big enough for Sinbad.

As the men pulled on their oars and sped swiftly into the darkness, Sinbad's raft was caught in a whirlpool!

The raft spun round and round then vanished, and poor Sinbad was tossed into the raging sea. Luckily by morning he had been washed up on a beach.

As he came to his senses Sinbad heard a hissing sound. Slithering across the beach was a huge serpent!

In fear for his life, Sinbad climbed to the top of the nearest tree with the serpent close behind.

By great good fortune, some sailors on a passing ship heard Sinbad's desperate cries. They sent a boat to pick him up and frightened off the serpent with a hail of arrows.

With Sinbad safely aboard, his rescuers listened in awe to his incredible story. Then, without any warning, a powerful wave dashed the ship against a jagged rock. Sinbad and the crew had scarcely time to jump off before the ship sank near an island.

The water was shallow, and when the men waded ashore, they discovered hundreds of chests overflowing with treasure – so many ships had been wrecked in that place and their valuable cargo washed up on the beach.

With all that treasure spread before them, the men could go home rich beyond their wildest dreams.

But unfortunately they had been shipwrecked at the foot of a high mountain with sides too steep to climb!

Sinbad was puzzled. A vast river of dark water flowed *from* the sea and disappeared through a cavern into the mountain.

"Could this be a means to escape?" wondered Sinbad.

When he explained to the men what he planned
to do, without a moment's hesitation, they gathered
up the ship's timber that littered the shore and built
a strong raft, and on top they loaded a cargo of
gold and precious stones.

"When I reach safety, I promise to send a ship for
you and the rest of the treasure!" called Sinbad as
he leapt aboard.

Swiftly the river took him through the mouth of
the cavern and deep into the mountain.

The water swept the raft along. Very soon Sinbad found himself in total darkness and after many hours he fell into a deep sleep.

When he awoke it was daylight. A group of people on the bank were surprised to see a stranger floating by. They tied his raft to a tree, and brought a fine horse for Sinbad to ride to the city of Serendib to meet the King.

The first thing the King did when he had listened to Sinbad's story was to send a ship to rescue the sailors still left behind.

During the days that followed, Sinbad and the King became great friends. And when Sinbad left for his own city, the King entrusted him with a letter of friendship and costly gifts for his ruler, the Caliph, so great was his faith in Sinbad.

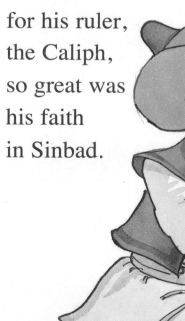

After a long journey Sinbad reached home. Straight away he delivered the letter and gifts to the Caliph, who was delighted.

"You must go back to the King of Serendib with gifts from me in return for his friendship."

So Sinbad was forced to set sail once more, as the Caliph could not be disobeyed. When he arrived in Serendib, the King was overjoyed to see Sinbad again, and was greatly honoured by the Caliph's gifts.

But alas, on the way home, Sinbad's ship was attacked by pirates!

They took the ship and all the treasure that had been loaded on board from the King of Serendib.

The pirates captured Sinbad and the crew and chained them up in the hold. Worse still, they were sold as slaves in the next port.

Sinbad was bought by a wealthy merchant and taken to join the rest of his many servants. Although he was now a slave, his life was not hard.

The merchant had a beautiful daughter named Yasmin, and as the time passed Sinbad fell in love with her.

One early morning the merchant sent for Sinbad. "Slave! I have a special task for you. In the forest lives the biggest of all elephants. Tonight, when the moon shines full, he will come to drink at the pool nearby. Take this bow and arrow and shoot him, or I will have you killed!"

Sinbad was horrified for he knew the merchant wanted the elephant's valuable ivory tusks to sell. What was he to do?

That night Sinbad set off towards the forest as the merchant had ordered.

On reaching the pool, Sinbad hid behind a large rock and waited. As he watched he saw the great elephant striding out of the forest. Its long curved tusks gleamed in the moonlight as it waded into the water.

Sinbad stepped forward cautiously, then he saw to his astonishment, the merchant's beautiful daughter sitting on the elephant. At first when Yasmin noticed Sinbad she was very upset.

"My father is a cruel man. That is why I come here at night to protect this gentle creature," she cried. "Shoot me instead! For I would rather die myself than let this beautiful elephant die!"

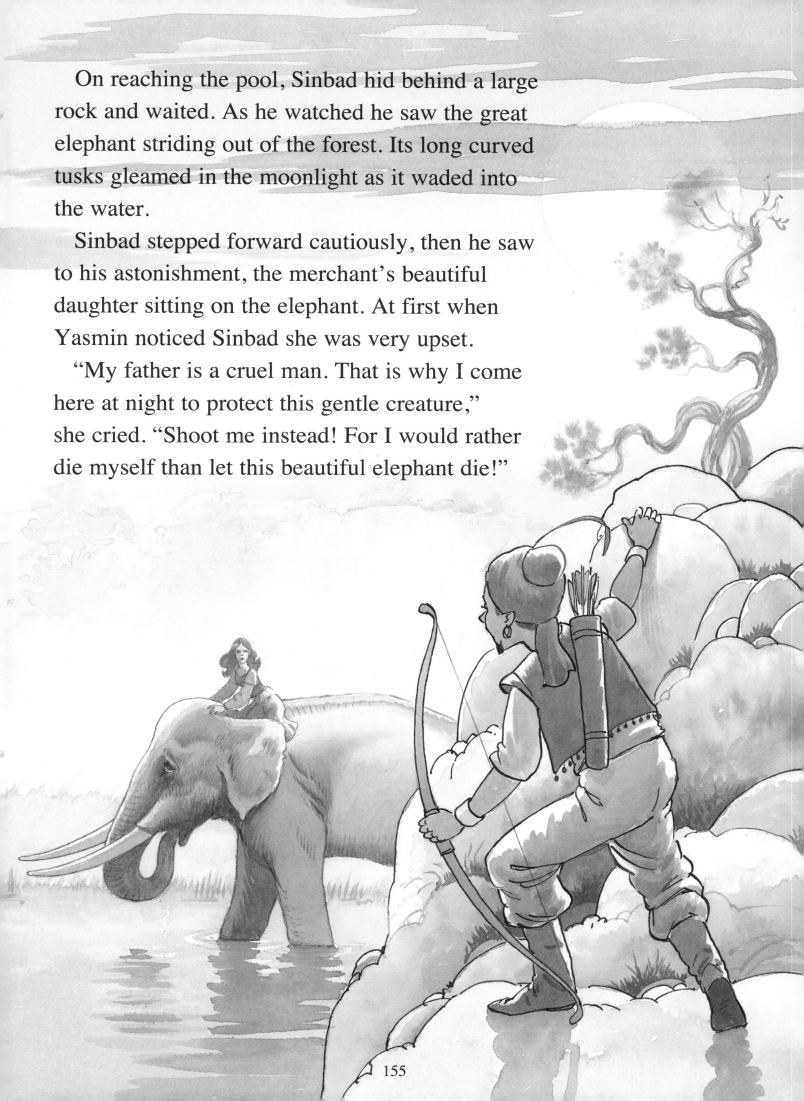

"Tonight I came to the pool to *save* the elephant," explained Sinbad. "I know your father is waiting for me to bring back its ivory tusks, but I planned to ride away on the elephant to freedom."

Yasmin had never felt happier in her life when she heard what Sinbad said, for now her beloved elephant would be saved from the cruellest of fates.

"I have no wish to return to my father," sighed Yasmin, "but where shall I go?"

"Come and live in my city," said Sinbad. Yasmin gladly agreed (for secretly she had fallen in love with him the moment he was brought to the house as a slave).

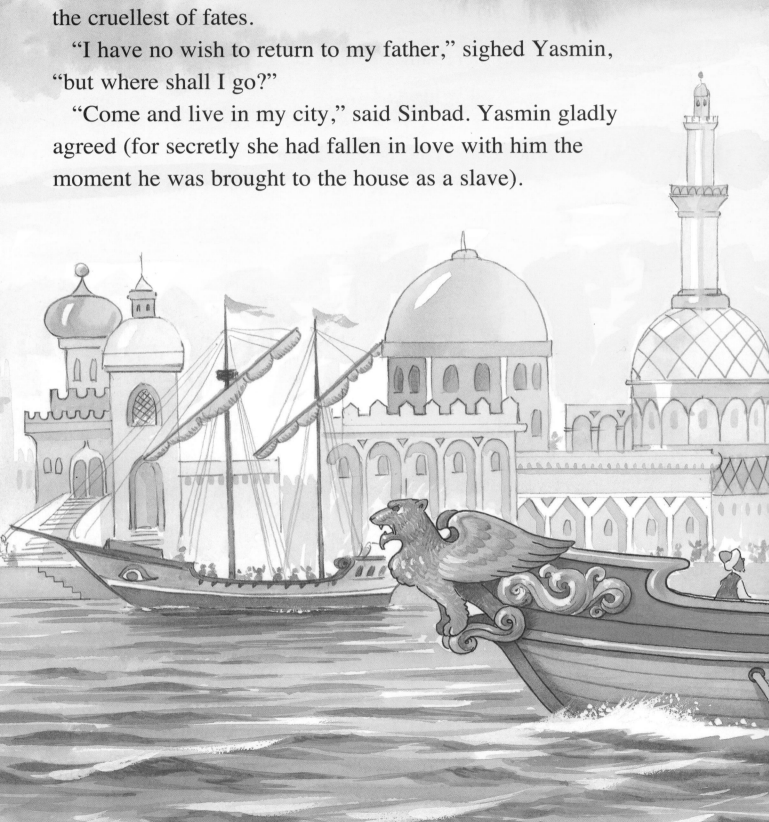

The two journeyed through many different lands, they travelled across hot deserts, wide plains and high mountains, but Yasmin and Sinbad were safe every step of the way on the back of their elephant.

When they came in sight of Sinbad's city, the Caliph's own barge was waiting to carry them across the water.

Great were the celebrations when people saw the golden barge arrive, for Sinbad had come home at last.

When tales of his incredible adventures were told, Sinbad became famous throughout the land.

He never put to sea again and gave most of the riches he had made from his voyages to the poor…and Yasmin and Sinbad lived happily ever after.

The End